THE DONKEY'S DAY OUT

Some time ago, when I was watching the television news, I saw a feature about a racehorse that was going to run in the Grand National — one of the most famous races in the world. The horse was a very nervous, moody animal and would not go anywhere without his special friend. This turned out to be, not a stable boy, or another horse, but a little grey donkey. Wherever the racehorse went the donkey went too, and it was now going to the Grand National itself, where its friend, the mighty black racehorse, was expected to win.

When the news was over I went on thinking about that donkey, and I began to wonder what would happen to it if its friend really *did* win. Would they stroke it and fuss it, take photographs, put flowers round its neck? Or would it be shut away in a horse-box somewhere, or left in a lonely field, while its friend got all the praise and glory?

Then I remembered "The Donkey", a poem I loved when I was young, which describes the "monstrous head and sickening cry" of that fat little stumpy creature which, on Palm Sunday, carried Jesus into Jerusalem.

I never found out what happened to the TV donkey, or whether his friend the racehorse won the Grand National, but I suddenly thought of another donkey, called Fred, and a friendship he had with a young horse called Tarquin. And that's where this story began . . .

Ann Pilling

ANN PILLING

The Donkey's Day Out

ILLUSTRATIONS BY

Sheila Ratcliffe

A LION PICTURE STORY

Oxford · Batavia · Sydney

Fred was the donkey at Hoggart's Farm. He shared his field with three cows called Polly, Molly and Joan, who all had black patches on their broad white backs. Fred had a cross on his. When he was a foal he'd asked his mother about it but she didn't know why. "All donkeys have them," she told him, peacefully munching thistles.

That was long ago, and now Fred was old. Sometimes, when Polly, Molly and Joan were having one of their special cow talks, he would stand and dream under the willow trees.

He would think about the awful morning when he had been taken from his mother and brought to Hoggart's in an old green horse-box. How frightened he had been that day, how lonely, and how he'd longed to leap across the broad blue river and go back to his old familiar field.

But then Mrs Hoggart had come to see him. She'd tied a big yellow bow round his neck, patted him and said kindly, "There, Fred, you look very handsome indeed. You're going to be a special birthday present for my son John."

John's birthday party was in the paddock, under the willow trees. There was cake and ice-cream for the children and a juicy red apple for Fred. When all the food had been eaten, everybody took turns at climbing on to his back and riding him up and down.

6

John was grown up now and they called him "Mr John". Everything was changing. Old Farmer Hoggart and his wife were moving to a cottage in the village and Mr John was getting rid of the farm animals to make room for horses. They would jump high fences and win gold and silver cups. Some special stable boys were coming to look after them.

One day Fred woke up from his after-dinner nap and saw Polly, Molly and Joan being driven out of the paddock. The space was needed for one of the new horses, and the cows had been sold to Farmer Hill up the lane.

It felt lonely without his friends, and Fred was frightened. If all the animals were going to new homes, *what would happen to him?*

Every time he saw Mr John, Fred ran and hid. Very soon that old green horse-box would stop by the gate. He would be pushed into it and driven away to another farm.

One morning a horse-box did arrive but it was shining white with silver wheels. Mr John and William, the chief stable boy, were leading something out of it.

It was a young horse, jet-black, and he looked very scared. Fred saw him plunge and kick and shy away as they tried to get him through the gate. As he reared up the sun gleamed on his glossy neck, and his terrified eyes flashed fire.

Then the two men walked across the grass. "Now," thought Fred, cowering away, "now they'll grab me and drive me off in that awful box." And he started to shake.

But he was wrong. William caught the black horse, soothed him and let him go while Mr John patted Fred's tubby sides. "Calm him down, old chap," he said. "He's a great jumper, but he's very nervous." And they went away.

Fred felt proud and happy. He wasn't going to be sold after all; he was staying to look after this young racehorse.

"What's your name?" he said, trotting up to him.

"Tarquin."

"That's a good name."

"It's the name of a king," the horse said proudly. "What's yours?"

"Er, Fred." It sounded silly, after "Tarquin".

The horse dropped his head and started to graze. They didn't talk any more then, but in the night Fred heard a little snuffling noise. Tarquin the Proud was crying.

"What's the matter?" asked Fred, snuggling up to him.

"I was dreaming about my mother. We were in a horse-box once. It crashed and she was killed. I miss her so much." And a tear rolled down his nose.

"Never mind," Fred said, "you've got me." To cheer him up he told him all about Hoggart's, and how he used to be Mr John's special pet, and how *he* didn't like horse-boxes either.

When the sun came up over the river they were still talking.

Tarquin and Fred were already firm friends.

In the long summer days, when the grass was thick and lush, the two lived happily together in the field by the river. But when the cold weather started Mr John caught Tarquin and William leaped on to his back.

"Winter quarters for you, my lad," he said. "Your stable's ready, all snug and warm. It's fit for a king in there. Come on."

But Tarquin wouldn't go when he saw that Fred had to stay behind and spend the winter in a broken-down shed. He bucked and reared and lashed out with his hooves till William fell off. Then he ran down to his friend, under the trees, nuzzling at his neck for comfort.

Three times William tried to mount Tarquin and three times he was thrown off.

At last he shook his head. "It's no good, Mr John," he said. "That donkey will have to come, too."

So Fred found himself walking behind Tarquin up the lane and into the new stable yard. From their stalls beautiful horses stared out at him, chestnut and white, and dapple-grey. But none of them was as beautiful as his own black Tarquin.

In their stable the straw was so deep it came up to his old knobbly knees, and there were food bags stuffed with sweet-smelling hay. There was even a heater for frosty nights. How different it was from his shack by the river, where mice scampered round his feet and gales blew through the cracks in the walls.

"Aren't you the lucky one, Fred?" said William, rubbing down Tarquin's glossy black coat. "This horse is going to be a real winner. He'll be running in big races one day."

Fred munched the wonderful hay and tried not to listen. Tarquin had already told him about the high hedges and fences he would have to jump, how the horses sometimes crashed into each other, how the riders limped home on crutches with their heads all bandaged. He didn't want his best friend to get hurt.

Next morning he heard the clatter of hooves outside. The stable boys were leading the horses round and round the yard. They had rugs on their backs and funny little hoods to keep their ears warm.

"Walkies, boys," shouted William, and they were off, away to the downs to canter and gallop and jump. In the cold air the breath from their nostrils puffed out like steam engines.

At first, Tarquin only ran in little races. Fred always stood nearby, in the yard, while they got him into the horse-box. Tarquin wouldn't go in unless Fred was there.

He ran so fast and he jumped so high that he won every single race. No one was prouder than the old grey donkey.

"Soon you'll be so grand you won't want to be friends with me any more," he said rather gloomily.

"Don't be silly," Tarquin told him. "You're my best friend."

When the spring came, Tarquin ran in his first big race. Mr John hired a very expensive horse-box and William was up before dawn, polishing and rubbing and grooming. When he'd finished, Tarquin's coat looked like a great black mirror. Fred stared at him in awe. He really did look like a king today.

They led Fred out and put him in the horse-box first. "*Me?*" he thought. "There must be some mistake." Then he heard Mr John whisper to the driver, "This is a difficult horse and the old donkey calms him down. We want to win the Junior Gold Cup today. I'm not taking any risks."

Tarquin whinnied with pleasure when he saw Fred. The special horse-box had thick padded sides, in case of sudden bumps and swerves. "Fit for a king," said Mr John proudly. And it was.

They talked all the way to the races, but when they arrived everybody forgot about Fred.

"Good luck," he said, as Tarquin was led off to be saddled and bridled. Then the horse-box was driven to the edge of a field and locked up.

All afternoon Fred strained his long ears to work out what was happening. It grew hot and a man came, gave him a bucket of water and let down the door of the box. But he still couldn't go to the races. He'd been tied up with a strong rope.

In the distance there were loud cheers, then it was quiet again. People wandered about, eating ice-creams and hot dogs. Once a child came up and patted Fred, but her mother pulled her away.

"It might bite," she said crossly. "Come on, we're here to see the horses, not a silly old donkey."

When at last Tarquin came back to the field there was a garland of flowers round his neck, and Mr John was carrying a gold cup. As they got Tarquin into the box hundreds of people came, cheering and clapping. "What a race!" they shouted. "What a champion!"

Fred was squashed into a corner to make room for another racehorse called Grey Prince. He was coming to live at Hoggart's, too.

Tarquin talked to the new horse all the way home. He never spoke to Fred, not even when the donkey whispered, "Well done."

It was all Grey Prince now, and the races, and his garland of flowers and his big gold cup. Fred kept trying to join in but the other two just ignored him.

"He's young," the donkey said to himself, "and he's had a great victory. That's why he wants to talk to his new friend." But inside, something was making him want to cry.

23

Now that Tarquin was a champion William kept him very busy running and jumping out on the hills, and he shared a new field with Grey Prince. Fred, still in the old paddock, never saw him at all and he felt very lonely. Tarquin didn't love him any more.

One afternoon two strange boys came up from the village, crept to the gate and looked all round. When they were sure that nobody was looking, they jumped into Fred's field and grabbed him. They had games to play.

One leaped on to the donkey's back, dug his heels into Fred's plump sides and went galloping round the paddock. "Gee up, you silly fool!" he yelled. "We're at the races! Can't you go any faster? No wonder you can't jump – your stomach's nearly touching the ground. You're an ugly beast you are, ugly and *fat*. Come *on*, can't you?"

Then the other boy joined in, running behind and slashing at Fred with a stick. "You're pathetic!" he shouted, as the donkey, sweating and panting, with his old heart pounding away like a great engine, lumbered round and round.

When he was young he could easily have thrown the boy off his back and chased the other one away. But he was too old now, too frightened and too weak.

"Giddy up, big head!" and "Giddy up, cloth ears!" they screamed gleefully as he trotted here and there, while the sharp heels dug into his sides and the thorny stick cut into his back.

When they were tired of running races they jumped over the gate and back into the lane. Now that he was safe again Fred let out a loud "Hee Haw".

"Ugly brute!" one of them yelled. The other picked up a stone and flung it at him. "Let's go and see Tarquin and Grey Prince," he said. "They run proper races, those two."

After they had gone Fred limped slowly away and hid under the trees. When he thought about what the two boys had done, he wept. It was the unhappiest day of his whole life.

But one morning, soon afterwards, William paid him a visit. "Come on, old chap," he said. "You're needed down in the village."

"Who needs *me*?" Fred thought sadly. He was ugly and old and fat. He had a great big head and a loud harsh voice. He was useless – just something to make fun of and throw stones at.

Anyway, he didn't really want to go to the village; he might see those boys. "Perhaps the milk van's broken down again," he thought, "and they want me to pull that old cart."

But they went straight past the milkman's house and stopped at the school. Lots of children were rushing about in bright robes. "Hello, Fred," someone shouted, and one of the teachers gave him a carrot.

Then they helped a little boy on to his back. He was dressed all in white and he had a long black beard made out of knitting wool. On his head was a crown made of shiny gold paper. "My name's Tom," he told Fred. "I've got the best part in our play. I'm Jesus."

It began with a story, and everybody crowded round. Fred nudged forward too. He liked stories. As he listened he knew it was the most important one he had ever heard.

The children were going to act the part called "Palm Sunday". It was about the wonderful day when Jesus rode into Jerusalem on a donkey. "Hosanna! Praise to Jesus!" all the people had shouted; then, "Behold, thy King cometh unto thee, meek and riding upon an ass." The beautiful old words made Fred's heart almost burst with joy. This was about *him*.